The Amazing Love Story

of Mr. Morf

Written and illustrated

by

Carll Cneut

Clarion Books • New York

Mr. Morf is a dog. Not a lapdog kind of dog. Not a "fetch my slippers" kind of dog. Not even a "get my newspaper" or a "guard the house" kind of dog.

Mr. Morf is a circus dog. He has a very important job. People come from far and wide to see him. Every day Mr. Morf practices walking across his tightrope, high up in the big top. He is very fast and very good. He stretches his right leg first . . . then his left leg . . . then off he goes!

Mr. Morf has been performing at the big top since puppyhood. Day after day after day.

But one day, Mr. Morf decided to stay in bed. "I don't feel well,"
he moaned. "I must be sick."

As he lay there, Mr. Morf thought about all his friends in the circus.
Igor and Brunhilde, the rolling bears: they were always so happy
together. Mr. and Mrs. Fred, the juggling duo: they were very fond of
each other as well. And Miranda and Melinda, the flying sisters on the
trapeze. They moved so fast it was hard to tell, but Mr. Morf was sure
they were very happy, too.

They all had each other and Mr. Morf had no one.
"I'm sick with loneliness," he sighed. "I need someone to love."

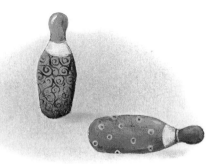

So Mr. Morf packed his bag, put on his Sunday hat, and left a note for the circus boss.

Dear Mr. Circus Boss,

Sadly, I must go away for an unspecified time.

Yours truly,
Walter Morf, Esq.

And off he went, to look for a friend to love.

He soon found a place where he felt at home.

"Penelope's the name," sang a swallow next to him. "I must admit I find your skills quite impressive. One doesn't see many dogs at this height."

Mr. Morf was excited to hear this. "Come away with me and be my friend," he said. "We'll play all day on the high wire, and at night I'll tell you stories." "I'm sorry, my dear," Penelope said. "My sisters and I are leaving today. We holiday abroad this time of year."

Penelope kissed his nose and, free as a bird, flew away.

Mr. Morf came to a hole in the ground.

"Is anyone there?" he called.

"I am," replied a mole.

"I'm looking for a friend," Mr. Morf said earnestly.

"Oh, lucky me!" said the mole. "I was feeling so sad and blue. Please wait for me. I'll pack my bags and see you up there."

Mr. Morf waited all day and night, until he heard a tiny, faraway voice.

"I've lost my way!" called the mole. "I'll never find you. It's so hard to see down here . . ."

Mr. Morf dug and dug, but there wasn't a soul to be seen. With a sigh, he picked up his bag and on he went.

Mr. Morf found a pig wallowing in the mud.

"How do you do?" said Mr. Morf. "I wonder if you'd like to play?"

"Certainly," she said. "Come on in. Oink! We'll have a ball."

"That's kind of you," said Mr. Morf, anxious about his Sunday hat, "but perhaps you'd prefer to come with me. We'll eat some cake and talk for hours. Then we'll jump through hoops and dance on the high wire from dawn till dusk."

"Oh, dear," she said. "Hoops and wires, you say? Oink! What a shame. And the cake sounded so nice."

"Then I will wish you a good day, madam," said Mr. Morf, and he left her to wallow.

Mr. Morf arrived at a tree where an owl was deeply asleep.

"ZZzzzzzZZZzzzzzZz," the owl snored.
And sometimes "OOooooooOOOoh." Then "ZZzzzzzZZZzzzzzZz" again.
"A very good day to you," Mr. Morf called. "Will you be my friend?"
The owl opened one eye and then the other. "Did someone speak? Ah, hello,
young man. I'm afraid I didn't hear a word you said. You see, we owls sleep
all day and stay up all night." He closed one eye and then the other.
"OOooooooOOOoh," he said. And "ZZzzzzzZZZzzzzzZz" again.

"Alas," said Mr. Morf. "He would have been such a wise friend." And he went on.

Mr. Morf came upon a cat on a roof.

"No, no, no, no, no!" said the cat.
Mr. Morf edged back along the roof. "I only wanted to be friends," he said.
"Friends?" said the cat. "You must be mad. You see," he went on, "we cats dislike dogs. Especially ones who walk on rooftops. In fact, we hate dogs!"

Mr. Morf was saddened by this attitude. Trembling a little, he bravely went on his way.

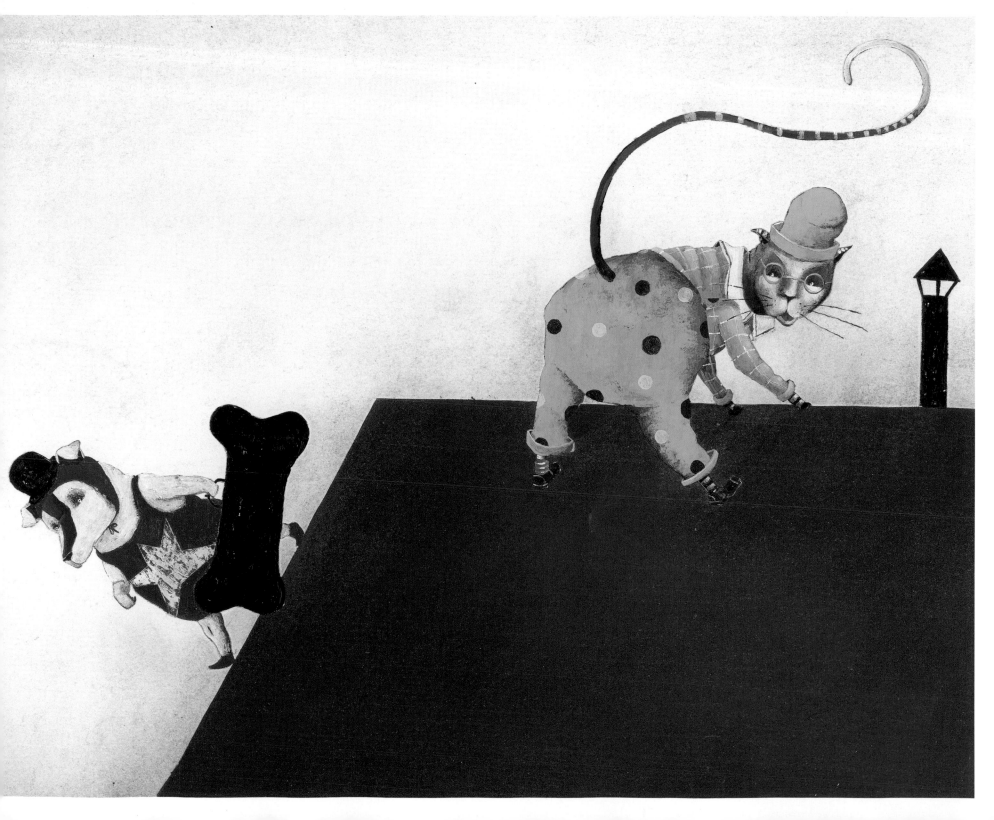

Mr. Morf went into a wood.

"Hello," said a wolf. "What a splendid surprise! I am glad to meet you. The other animals won't stop and talk, you know. One gets quite lonely."

"Perhaps it's because you have such big ears," said Mr. Morf.

"All the better to hear you with, my dear," said the wolf.

"Then perhaps it's because you have such big eyes," said Mr. Morf.

"All the better to see you with," said the wolf.

"Or perhaps," said Mr. Morf, "it's because you have such big teeth."

"All the better to eat you with," said the wolf. And he opened his mouth to bite.

Luckily, Mr. Morf was too quick for him. He ran up a tree and jumped from branch to branch until he was safe.

Brokenhearted, Mr. Morf decided to go back to the circus.

Then, suddenly, after days and weeks of searching in vain, he started to smile. Then he started to giggle. Before long, he was laughing fit to burst. Something was tickling him. It tickled so much that he couldn't eat or sleep, and his giggles echoed all round the big top.

Doctors, pharmacists, and all sorts of healers came from here, there, and everywhere to examine Mr. Morf. Some thought he'd lost his mind. Others suggested he'd gone mad with loneliness.

Finally, a wise old street dog said, "I know what it is. He's got a flea!"

So tiny, so sweet, and oh! so very different, only a flea could tickle
Mr. Morf to bits.

"Will you be my friend," Mr. Morf asked the flea, "and stay with me forever?"
"There's nothing I'd rather do," giggled Isabella (for that was her name).
"I'll stay forever and a day."